The Night Baa fore Christmas

Written by Dawn Young

Illustrated by Pablo Pino

WORTHY® kids

To Mom and Dad,
thanks for everything.
I love ewe! —D.Y.

To Agos, who taught me
how to count many,
many sheep. —P.P.

ISBN: 978-1-5460-1458-4

WorthyKids
Hachette Book Group
1290 Avenue of the Americas
New York, NY 10104

Text copyright © 2019 by Dawn Young
Art copyright © 2019 by Hachette Book Group, Inc.

Library of Congress CIP data on file

Designed by Eve DeGrie
Printed and bound in China
RRD-S
10 9 8 7 6 5 4 3 2 1

Tossing and turning...

Bo can't fall asleep.
He sits up in bed and he calls out,

"Hey, sheep!
Tonight's Christmas Eve
and I'd like a new drum,

but if I'm not sleeping,
then Santa won't come."

They jump and Bo counts, but with Bo *still* awake,
the sheep go on strike
and demand a short break.

They're puffing and panting.
Bo tells them, "Okay,
I'll bring you a drink
if you promise to
STAY!"

They nod, but the minute Bo slips out the door,
they tiptoe behind and spot goodies galore!

Dashing and darting,
they scatter like mice.

They slip and they slide,
like the floor's made of ice.

They skid toward the tree, and then, in a flash,
it tilts and it tips,
and it topples down—
CRASH!

While Bo saves the angel, **sheep 1**, **2**, and **3** nibble nonstop to the top of the tree.

Sheep 4 gnaws the stockings,
leaves holes in the toes.
5 swallows some garland
and ribbon and bows!

Bo dangles some carrots
to lure them his way,
but they find the fridge
and they bellow

"baa-ffet!"

6 eats Santa's cookies, while **7** and **8**

chew up Bo's letter and chomp down the plate.

9 drools as he munches—there's green in his teeth.

Bo races to rescue his mother's new wreath.

"Let's go," insists Bo, "so I'm nestled in bed
while visions of sugarplums
dance through my head."

When **10** hears the word "dance," ...

he gets the whole flock
to wiggle their wool
   to the "Jingle Bell Rock"!

They ring and they swing
   and they cha-cha on chairs,
then carol and conga
   and head for the stairs.

Bo knows to move fast,
'cause they're out of control.
"If Santa sees this,
I'll get nothing but coal!"

Bo reads them a story.
They listen and look

till **10** licks a page,
then devours the book.

Sheep 9, scared of monsters, hides under the rug,

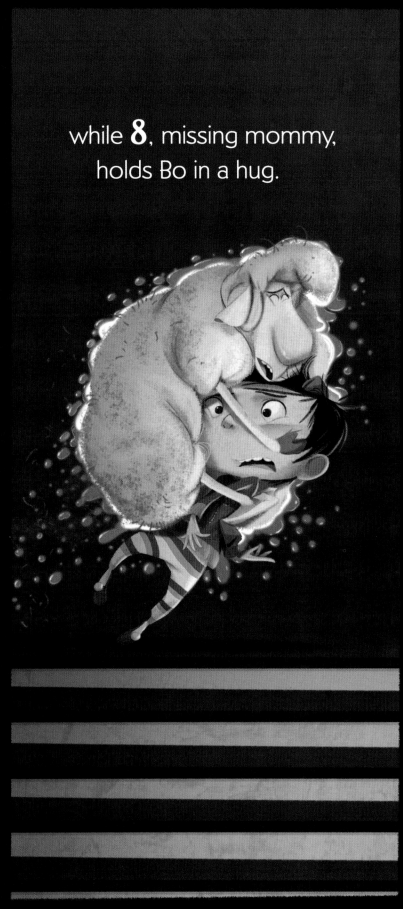

while **8**, missing mommy, holds Bo in a hug.

Bo tries what his mom does—
he sings lullabies.
As soon as she hears them,
sheep 7 just cries.

Then **6** wrestles **5**,
who's refusing to share,
parading around
in his new underwear.

Bo dims all the lights, and he rubs the flock's fleece.
But right when Bo thinks he might finally have peace,

4 sneaks up and swipes the remote from sheep **3**.
Both wail when Bo tells them,

"You **can't** watch TV!"

Sheep 2 throws a tantrum
'cause **1** took his bear
and hid it someplace—
but he can't recall where.

Bo panics. It's late, and for Santa to come,
Bo has to be sleeping, or else...there's no drum.

With Santa en route and with so much to do,
Bo scurries to round up each ram and each ewe.

"There's **1**, and there's **2**.
I see **3**, and there's **4**.
There's **5**, **6**, and **7**.
There's **8**, and . . ."

They snore.
Bo counted the sheep—
but he put them to sleep!

And he's got a mess
left to pick up
and sweep.

Bo lugs all the sheep
down the hall to his room . . .

then cleans as he counts
every swish of the broom.

"Dear Santa,
   They're tucked in.
It's clean, so please come.

"And don't forget, Santa,
   I'd love a new . . .